MATZOH
MOUSE

by Lauren L. Wohl

Illustrated by Pamela Keavney

jW815M

A Charlotte Zolotow Book
An Imprint of
HarperCollins*Publishers*

Matzoh Mouse
Text copyright © 1991 by Lauren L. Wohl
Illustrations copyright © 1991 by Pamela Keavney
Printed in the U.S.A. All rights reserved.
1 2 3 4 5 6 7 8 9 10
First Edition

Library of Congress Cataloging-in-Publication Data
Wohl, Lauren.
  Matzoh Mouse / Lauren Wohl ; pictures by Pamela Keavney.
      p.   cm.
  "A Charlotte Zolotow book."
  Summary: While helping her parents prepare for the Passover seder,
nine-year-old Sarah cannot resist nibbling on the chocolate-covered
matzoh.
  ISBN 0-06-026580-9.—ISBN 0-06-026581-7 (lib. bdg.)
  [1. Passover—Fiction.]   I. Keavney, Pamela, ill.   II. Title.
PZ7.W818564Mat   1991   90-31976
[E]—dc20   CIP
                                                              AC

For my parents—
It's just now that I see your constant love
and gentle understanding

L.L.W.

To Jim, for all your encouragement,
with love,

P.K.

The winter Sarah was nine was cold—very cold. And long—*very* long!

It was not until the end of March that Sarah finally saw signs of spring in the thickening branches of the trees, in the tiny shoots of yellow and purple crocuses just breaking through the earth, and in her parents' sudden passion for housecleaning.

Through the last week of March and the first week of April, they swept every inch of every room spotless. Mattresses were vacuumed and turned. Shades and blinds were removed and bathed in the tub. Curtains came down, were washed, and starched and ironed, then rehung. Carpets were shampooed, and furniture was moved and dusted from every angle.

Sarah's job was to clean out the mess on the floor of the hall closet. When she was done, every boot stood next to its mate; every umbrella was neatly folded and tied shut. And Sarah cleaned out her own dresser drawers, folding sweaters, matching socks, and organizing blouses according to their colors. She straightened out the music in the piano bench, too.

"Look!" she said to her mother.

"Thank you, Sarah." Her mother leaned down and kissed her. "Thank you."

When all but the kitchen and dining room were cleaned, Sarah's mother went shopping. She brought home two cartons of food and put them behind the big club chair in the living room, marked:

FOR PASSOVER. DO NOT TOUCH!

The warning was for Sarah.

Over the next two weeks, Sarah often sat backward in the big chair and peered over the headrest into those cartons at the boxes of candy, and bags of nuts, the jars, the cans, the tins of spices—and she counted the days until the first seder, the festival meal, when these would be served.

Sometimes Sarah leaned all the way over the back of the chair and breathed in as deeply as she could. The sharp smell of the cinnamon made her mouth water.

Sometimes Sarah walked behind the chair and sat between the two big boxes and sniffed the coconutty smell of the macaroons.

And sometimes she stuck her head into one of the boxes, and the rich aroma of the chocolate-covered matzoh was so clear—so strong—that she could almost taste it!

But she remembered her mother's clear printing on the side of each carton:

FOR PASSOVER. DO NOT TOUCH!

And she didn't.

When there were only five days to go until the first seder night, and Sarah's parents were busy with last-minute kitchen preparations, Sarah decided to help them by reorganizing the goodies in the cartons. This wouldn't be *touching*; this would be *helping*!

She walked behind the big club chair, sat down quietly, and removed everything from the larger carton. Out came the marshmallow twists, the jelly slices, the macaroons, and then the chocolate-covered matzoh, her favorite of the Passover sweets. Yummm…

The temptation was overwhelming.

Sarah gave in.

Carefully, she opened the box and broke off a square of the candy. She rested it on the arm of the chair and returned the package to the carton, tossing in the other foods, too.

She carried her prize to her bedroom and ate it—little pieces at a time. She sucked the chocolate off first; then she crunched the matzoh, licked her fingers clean, and finally swept the crumbs from her bed into her palm and ate the last bits.

Her parents were still busy in the kitchen. And, Sarah remembered, she hadn't straightened out the cartons at all. So back she went, back behind the club chair. Out came the goodies.

But instead of straightening the boxes, Sarah helped herself to a whole section of the chocolate-covered matzoh, wrapped it in a tissue, and carried it to her room. She waited until bedtime and ate it bite by bite.

Three days later Sarah's mother asked her to bring the food from behind the chair into the kitchen. The applesauce and juices should go into the refrigerator, the spices should be placed on the freshly lined shelf of the pantry, and the cans should be lined up on the counter where the toaster usually stood. The sweets should remain in the living room, if Sarah would please put them all in one box and throw the empty carton away.

Sarah took the long, skinny box of after-dinner mints out of the small carton and placed it along the bottom of the larger one. Then she broke off a piece of chocolate-covered matzoh and ate it. Sarah moved the short, fat box of marshmallow twists and rested it sidewise in the larger carton. And then she took another corner of chocolate-covered matzoh and ate it. She grabbed the cellophane bag of hard candies and stuffed it into a corner of the larger carton. She took another piece of chocolate-covered matzoh and ate it. She pushed the bags of nuts into an empty corner. And then she took a final piece of chocolate-covered matzoh and ate it.

As Sarah put the box of chocolate-covered matzoh back into the carton, it felt very light. She shook it gently. It sounded as if there were only one piece in the package. That couldn't be. She opened the box and looked in. There *was* only one small piece left. Had she really eaten all the rest? Did that mean that no one else would have a piece as an after-seder treat? And what would her parents think?

Sarah resealed the box carefully. No one could tell it had been opened. She put it in the center of the carton.

"All done," Sarah called to her mother.

"Thanks again, dear."

The seder was especially festive that year. Sarah's only younger cousin, Vicki, was finally old enough to ask the four questions.

"Why is this night different from all other nights?"

Sarah was chosen to start the telling of the answer. "We were slaves of the Pharaoh in Egypt," she began reading, "and the Eternal our God brought us out from there with a strong hand and an outstretched arm." Each relative read from the Haggadah, telling more of the story of the Jews' exodus from slavery.

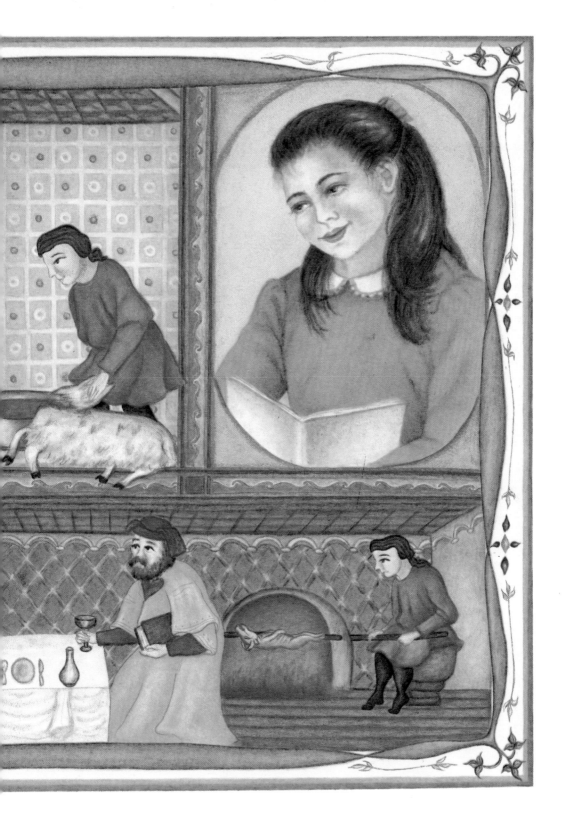

עֶשֶׂר מַכֹּת

Cousin Marty recited the ten plagues that fell on Egypt—blood, frogs, vermin, and beasts; cattle disease, boils, hail, and locusts; darkness and the slaying of the firstborn. Everyone at the table spilled a drop of wine for each of the plagues named. Sarah shuddered.

Cousin Lee explained the symbols on the seder plate: the horseradish to remind everyone of the bitterness of slavery; the parsley to recall the season of the year; the sweet-tasting nuts-apple-and-wine mixture called haroseth, symbolizing the mortar Jewish slaves used for building the Pharaoh's pyramids and cities; the matzoh, the bread that had no time to rise when Moses rushed his people out of Egypt to freedom.

Sarah's favorite part of the seder soon arrived. Her father asked her to open the door for the prophet Elijah and welcome him in to share their family's seder. Carol, the most musical of the cousins, led the singing as Sarah slowly walked to the front door and opened it. The wind was strong. The screen door blew open wide, out of Sarah's grasp. A gust blew through the house, convincing everyone that Elijah really had come to their seder so that from this Passover to the next, each of them would have a year that had been truly blessed.

After dinner and after singing, the children began their search for the afikomen—the dessert piece of matzoh Sarah's father had hidden. The children would get a prize for finding it. They began their search on their own but were unsuccessful. "Hot or cold," they begged. "Are we hot or cold?" they yelled as they moved from room to room.

"Hot, hot, burning hot," Sarah's father told them when they reached the bookcase at the top of the stairs. "You're going to melt if you don't find it soon." And there it was, wrapped in a dinner napkin, on top of the books on the third shelf.

"We found it." Marty negotiated for the group. "What will you give us for it?"

Sarah's father was prepared. There was a book for each of them, especially chosen, especially wrapped.

The adults in the living room talked about the delicious meal and told stories of other Passovers—stories told and retold every time the family got together.

Sarah's mother was in the kitchen, setting out trays of fruits and nuts and candy. She carried these into the living room and asked Sarah to make room for them on the coffee table.

Suddenly Sarah remembered the box of chocolate-covered matzoh.

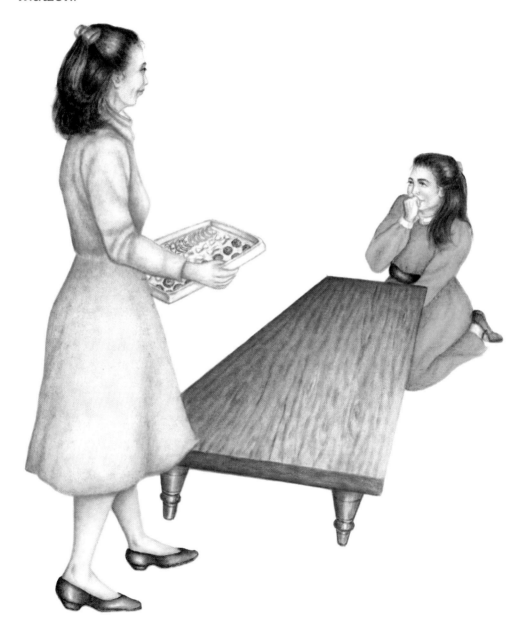

Sarah's aunts and uncles and cousins all sat forward, leaning toward the coffee table as the sweets were set before them.

There, on the tray, were marshmallow twists, mints, jelly slices, macaroons, almonds, cashews, walnuts, and raisins.

But there was no chocolate-covered matzoh!

"Where is the chocolate-covered matzoh?" Uncle Sid asked. "It's Sarah's favorite."

"Her father's favorite too, when we were little," Aunt Anne said. She smiled at her brother.

"Funny thing," Sarah's mother said. "I bought a box, but when I opened it tonight, there was only one tiny piece of candy in it—stuck to the bottom."

"That's odd," Sarah's father said.

"Maybe you've got a mouse," Aunt Anne suggested. "A matzoh mouse," she added, looking at Sarah's father and smiling again.

"A matzoh mouse, huh?" Sarah's father nodded. Then he smiled too. "We had one when I was Sarah's age. I remember."

"Yes," Aunt Anne said. "It was a clever little mouse. It didn't just chew its way into the chocolate matzoh boxes. It opened them—neatly."

"Our box was opened neatly," Sarah's mother said.

"I guess that's it, then," Sarah's father said. "We've got ourselves a matzoh mouse."

Everyone went home at about nine. There were lots of hugs and laughter at the door. Aunt Anne gave Sarah's father an extra-long good-bye hug. Sarah helped her parents with the last of the cleanup chores. No one said anything. It seemed very quiet.

Finally Sarah said, "I have to tell you something."
Her father and mother looked at each other and smiled.
"Never mind," her father said gently. "We know."
Sarah looked at him.
He put his arm around her and kissed the top of her head.

"Good night, little matzoh mouse," he said. "Happy Passover."

And now, for Sarah, it really was!